‖‖‖‖‖ ‖‖‖‖‖‖‖‖‖‖‖‖‖‖‖‖‖

✧ **W9-CET-864**

YOU JUMP OFF THE LEDGE AND INTO THE WATER . . .

It is higher than your knees, and you struggle to run. The witch follows you, her cackling laugh echoing off the walls of the tunnel.

Just as you reach the exit and step out into the light, you feel the witch's hand grab your shoulder.

You turn to look at her and are very surprised at what you see.

"You don't look like a witch at all!" you exclaim. "You look just like a regular person."

"Don't move, my pretty, and I will prove to you that I am a witch."

If you stay to see the proof, turn to page 37.

If you walk away from the witch and go on to the Hall of Mirrors, turn to page 17.

BUT BE CAREFUL— THE FUTURE IS YOURS TO DECIDE!

WHICH WAY BOOKS for you to enjoy

Available from ARCHWAY paperbacks

Most Archway Paperbacks are available at special quantity discounts for bulk purchases for sales promotions, premiums or fund raising. Special books or book excerpts can also be created to fit specific needs.

For details write the office of the Vice President of Special Markets, Pocket Books, 1230 Avenue of the Americas, New York, New York 10020.

WHICH WAY BOOKS #3

THE SPELL OF THE BLACK RAVEN

R.G. Austin

ILLUSTRATED BY ANTHONY KRAMER

AN ARCHWAY PAPERBACK
Published by POCKET BOOKS • NEW YORK

AN ARCHWAY PAPERBACK *Original*

An Archway Paperback published by
POCKET BOOKS, a Simon & Schuster division of
GULF & WESTERN CORPORATION
1230 Avenue of the Americas, New York, N.Y. 10020

Text copyright © 1982 by R.G. Austin
Illustrations copyright © 1982 by Simon & Schuster,
a division of Gulf & Western Corporation

All rights reserved, including the right to reproduce
this book or portions thereof in any form whatsoever.
For information address Pocket Books, 1230 Avenue
of the Americas, New York, N.Y. 10020

ISBN: 0-671-47374-3

First Archway Paperback printing January, 1982

10 9 8 7 6 5 4 3

AN ARCHWAY PAPERBACK and colophon are
trademarks of Simon & Schuster.

WHICH WAY is a trademark of Simon & Schuster.

Printed in the U.S.A.

IL 3+

For Michelle

Attention!

Which Way Books must be read in a special way. DO NOT READ THE PAGES IN ORDER. If you do, the story will make no sense at all. Instead, follow the directions at the bottom of each page until you come to an ending. Only then should you return to the beginning and start over again, making different choices this time.

There are many possibilities for exciting adventures. Some of the endings are good; some of the endings are bad. If you meet a terrible fate, you can reverse it in your next story by making new choices.

Remember: follow the directions carefully, and have fun!

It is Saturday morning, and you have nothing to do. Even television seems boring. You know that tomorrow will be better, because it is your birthday.

When the postman arrives, you are surprised to receive a letter from your Uncle George. You have not seen him since you were three years old. He is an anthropologist and has been living with a tribe of Indians in some isolated mountains thousands of miles away.

You open the letter, hoping your uncle will tell you about the work he is doing. But instead, there is just a short note.

"Happy Birthday," it reads. "Since you are growing up so fast, I have decided to send you a very special gift this year. I am sure you will take good care of it.

"The Indians here say that the gift holds within it the special magic of the mountains. That is for you to decide. All I know is that it is extraordinary. I hope you think so, too.

"With love from your Uncle George."

That afternoon, just as you are about to go to a carnival, a special messenger delivers a large square box with round holes in the top.

(continued on page 2)

This must be Uncle George's gift, you think as you untie the string and remove the top.

You are shocked when a huge black bird sticks his head out of the box.

The tag around his leg reads: "I am a raven. My name is George, too."

As soon as you finish reading the note, the raven hops onto your shoulder. Suddenly, you feel strange and light-headed, as though a closed door in your mind has been thrown open. But when the raven leaves your shoulder, the feeling passes.

If you do not think that wild animals should be kept as pets, and you want to let the raven go before you become attached to him, turn to page 3.

If you decide to take George to the carnival with you, turn to page 5.

You take George in your hand and hold·him up high. Then, with a sweeping movement of your arm, you release him.

(continued on page 4)

Sadly, you watch him fly away. But he does not go far. Soon, he is back on your shoulder.

You try again and again. Each time George flies a bit farther away and then returns. You do not know what to do.

If you decide to go inside your house in the hope that, once you are out of sight, George will fly away, turn to page 6.

If you decide to introduce George to your friend, Papa John, who lives at the junkyard, turn to page 7.

George seems happy flying next to you as you stroll along the midway of the carnival. The smell of caramel apples and cotton candy fills the air.

You love carnivals. There are so many things to do, you do not know which to do first.

If you want to go to the House of Horrors, turn to page 10.

If you want to go to the Fun House, turn to page 11.

A few minutes later, you peer out of your window from behind the curtains. You are surprised to see that George is perched on the fencepost by your front gate.

You walk outside, and George hops onto your shoulder. You are astounded when you discover that George is holding the penknife that you lost more than two months ago when you were fishing.

Turn to page 12.

You climb onto your bike, and George hops on the handlebars. You pedal furiously to the junkyard. You know Papa John will be interested in the raven, because he has often talked to you about his own mystical powers. Something compels you to hurry.

When you arrive, you knock on the door of Papa John's shack. But there is no answer.

(continued on page 9)

Opening the door quietly, you look inside. Papa John is there. His eyes are closed; he is perfectly still.

"What's the matter?" you ask.

He opens his eyes slowly. "I've seen it!" he exclaims. "I've seen the past. And there is a message in it for us. But I don't know where or what it could be."

At that moment, George flutters his wings and flies to the center of a huge mound of junk. He picks up a dirty sheaf of papers in his beak and gives them to you. You see that they are part of a diary.

The papers are old and blurred. Only the last page can be read. "I fear my time has come," the diary reads. "The entire town is against me now. They taunt me, calling me the Raven Witch because of my black hair. They do not understand that my powers are nothing more than a sixth sense. Soon, they will come and take me away. I fear that my fate lies in the tunnel. I hope that someday someone will clear my name. I am innocent."

"That's it!" cries Papa John. "The message from the past. We've been chosen."

Turn to page 13.

You stroll to the end of the midway and buy a ticket for the House of Horrors. Then you climb into a little boat that takes you on a winding river-track through the house.

Skeletons drop down; ghosts float above your head; hysterical screams fill the air.

Turn to page 15.

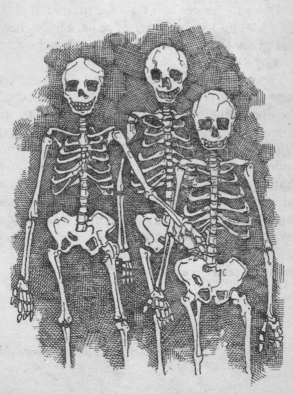

You walk into the Fun House. Everything you see is tempting.

Finally, you make a choice.

If you choose to ride down the Serpentine Slide, turn to page 16.

If you choose to go into the Hall of Mirrors, turn to page 17.

As you are standing there with George on your shoulder, a man begins to step off the curb in front of your house.

"Stop!" you yell at the top of your lungs.

The man turns to look at you; and, at that very moment, a speeding car skids around the corner. The man would have been killed if he had stepped into the street.

"Hey, kid," the man asks, "how d'ja do that? You couldn'a seen that car comin'."

"I don't know," you answer. "I just saw a picture in my mind of what would happen."

The man reaches into his pocket and pulls out something. His fist is closed. "What do I got in my hand?" he asks.

"An 1890 silver dollar," you answer, astonished that you know.

"The name's Rocco, kid," he says. "I got a job for you, and it pays good. Ya want it?"

If you accept the man's offer, turn to page 18.

If you refuse his offer, turn to page 19.

"What do you mean?" you ask excitedly. "Do you think this diary is true?"

"I certainly do," says Papa John. "Folks haven't changed all that much over the years. People have always been afraid of things they don't understand. That's the reason I never tell anybody about some of the things I see."

"Like what?" you ask, puzzled.

"Oh, sometimes I see things from the past, like today, and sometimes I see things that will happen in the future.

"I don't advertise the fact, mind you. People wouldn't understand, and they'd call me crazy just to cover up their fear."

(continued on page 14)

"What about the tunnel?" you ask.

"Folks used to talk about an old tunnel that went out from the middle of town to the beach. In the old days, it was used for smuggling."

"Do you think the writer of the diary was killed in the tunnel?"

"I don't know. But that diary was in a pile of junk that was taken out of Mrs. Bagely's attic after she died. Maybe you should go talk to Mrs. Bagely's sister, Mrs. Crabbe. She's a crotchety lady, but I think she'd be willing to talk to you. I hear they had an ancestor who was accused of being a witch. She's probably the one who wrote the diary."

If you want to go down to the beach and look for an entrance to the tunnel, turn to page 21.

If you want to talk to Mrs. Crabbe, turn to page 22.

A witch bobs back and forth over the water. You glance up just in time to see the witch's hands reach out to grab you.

The witch yanks you out of the boat and forces you onto a ledge.

If you scream, turn to page 23.

If you jump into the water and try to run away, turn to page 24.

You stand at the top of the slide, thinking that it looks forbiddingly high. Then you sit on a small rug and shove off.

George flies over your head doing aerial acrobatics—loop-the-loops and tailspins—as he tracks you on your way down the slide.

Around and around you go, laughing and squealing at the same time, loving every minute of it.

When you reach the bottom, you climb up the stairs and do it again. And then again and again.

Finally, after your fifth time, you hear an announcement on the loudspeaker:

"Ladies and gentlemen: come to the circus! The show is about to begin. Come now and get your tickets for the greatest show on earth. There are clowns and elephants, horses and tigers. There are trapeze artists and marching bands. Something for everybody. Come one; come all!"

Turn to page 25.

George rides on your shoulder as you enter the Hall of Mirrors. The mirrors are curved and bumpy, slanted and upside down. They make you look so funny that you begin to laugh.

Then you walk through a door and find yourself in a maze of mirrors. Everywhere you look, you see yourself and George.

George is confused. He flies around in circles, crowing, crying and bumping his head against the mirrors. You try to catch him, but you, too, are confused.

Suddenly a man appears.

"Let me help you," he says. "Follow me. I'll carry your bird."

If you go with the man, turn to page 26.

If you refuse the man's help, turn to page 27.

You are astonished at what you have just done and decide that it would be terrific if you could use your new power to earn some money.

"It's a deal," you say, shaking hands with the man.

"Good," the man says. "Get rid of the pigeon and come with me."

If you refuse to leave without George, turn to page 19.

If you tell Rocco to wait for you while you put George in the house, turn to page 28.

"This oughta make you change your mind," Rocco says as he pulls a pistol out of his pocket. He pushes George off your shoulder and says, "Move it!"

Rocco directs you to a candy store two blocks away, and you walk inside. But instead of stopping in the store, you go through a small door at the back and enter a crowded room. There is a huge amount of money in the middle of the floor, stacked in neat piles of five-, ten- and twenty-dollar bills. *There must be a million dollars in that pile of money,* you think.

(continued on page 20)

"There's a race in five minutes," Rocco says. "Here's a list of the horses. Tell me who's gonna win."

You look at the list, but no pictures come into your mind.

If you tell Rocco that you don't know the answer, turn to page 29.

If you look at the pistol and decide that a guess is a better answer than nothing, turn to page 47.

George rides on your handlebars. You remember that there are some caves in the rocky cliffs above the sand.

Just as you begin your climb toward the largest of the caves, George flies away.

If you follow George, turn to page 30.

If you continue climbing toward the cave, turn to page 31.

George flies with you as you approach Mrs. Crabbe's house. When Mrs. Crabbe answers the door, you explain the reason for your visit and read her the papers from the diary.

When you finish, Mrs. Crabbe looks at you strangely. "That diary must have been written by Rachel, one of my early ancestors," Mrs. Crabbe says. "She was seventeen when she died. Her story has always been a shameful family secret. We never talk about it."

Suddenly, George lands on your shoulder and you have that strange feeling again. In your head, you see a fireplace and a sliding wall panel. You describe it to Mrs. Crabbe, and she takes you to the back parlor, where you see the identical scene. But this time it is real.

You inspect the panel carefully. Then, with a push, you slide open the panel and expose a narrow staircase leading down into darkness.

If you borrow Mrs. Crabbe's flashlight and go down the stairs, turn to page 32.

If you tell Mrs. Crabbe that you are going to go get Papa John to help you explore, turn to page 33.

It is pitch black. You try to scream, but a cold clawlike hand clamps over your mouth.

The witch drags you down a long corridor and into a dimly lit room. Dark figures move in the shadows. The only light comes from a fire in a fireplace. A hunched figure bends over a cauldron that is suspended from a heavy hook above the flames.

Witches and warlocks chant confusing words in a low, persistent hum.

The witch walks over to the steaming pot in the fireplace. As she dips into it, the contents hiss and bubble.

She serves you some of the contents of the cauldron in a small bowl. "Here, my pretty," she says with a hideous grin, "have something to eat."

If you refuse to eat, turn to page 35.

If you decide that it would be better to cooperate, turn to page 36.

You jump off the ledge and into the water. It is higher than your knees, and you struggle to run. The witch follows you, her cackling laugh echoing off the walls of the tunnel.

Just as you reach the exit and step out into the light, you feel the witch's hand grab your shoulder.

You turn to look at her and are very surprised at what you see.

"You don't look like a witch at all!" you exclaim. "You look just like a regular person."

"Don't move, my pretty, and I will prove to you that I *am* a witch."

If you stay to see the proof, turn to page 37.

If you walk away from the witch and go on to the Hall of Mirrors, turn to page 17.

You are thrilled to get a front-row seat in the giant tent. You watch as George flies overhead and does tricks for the audience. Finally, he comes to rest on your shoulder.

All of a sudden, you get that same dizzy feeling that you had when George landed on your shoulder for the first time. And then, to your horror, you see a picture in your mind of a fire in the circus tent. It is near the bandstand.

You shake your head, trying to get rid of the picture; but instead, it becomes even more vivid.

Finally, you realize that the magic raven is trying to tell you that soon there will be a fire in this very tent.

You do not know what to do.

If you lean over and whisper to the clown who is dancing in front of you that there is going to be a fire in the tent, turn to page 38.

If you want to explore the area around the bandstand, turn to page 40.

The man carries George under his arm as he leads you out of the maze and onto the midway. You are relieved to be out of the House of Mirrors and ask the man if there is anything you can do to return the favor.

"There is something," he says thoughtfully. "Will you deliver this letter to a house not far from here?"

"Of course," you answer, happy to oblige.

Turn to page 41.

"I can get out of here myself," you say stubbornly to the stranger. *Besides,* you think, *I don't like the way you look.*

"Give me the bird," the man orders, moving toward you.

You run around the next corner, holding George under your arm. You can hear the man chasing you, but all you can see is the reflection of you and George in every direction you look. You keep bumping into mirrors, turning corners and bumping into more mirrors.

Finally, you come to a door and open it. You are relieved to see that you are once again outside.

If you have had enough of the carnival for one day and would like to go show George to your friend Papa John, who lives at the junkyard, you may go home now and get your bike. Turn to page 7.

If you want to ride on the bumper cars, turn to page 42.

You run into the house, carrying George with you. As soon as you are inside, you become suspicious, and suddenly you know that you never should have agreed to go with the man.

You race through your house and out the back door.

"We're going to the carnival," you tell George. "And we're not going with anybody else."

Turn to page 5.

"I don't know," you say, frightened.

"Hey, Ratso," Rocco calls to a huge man with a mashed-in nose and cauliflower ears. "Help convince the kid here that there's a way to remember these things."

The man moves toward you and raises his fist. Just as he is about to swing, George flies in the window and perches on your shoulder.

Suddenly, a picture flashes into your mind, and you know that the horse named Elmer will win the race.

You realize that you will be helping criminals if you tell the truth. But Ratso and his pistol have suddenly become very convincing.

If you tell Ratso and Rocco that Elmer will win the race, turn to page 44.

If you think lying would be better than helping Rocco and his friends, turn to page 47.

You run back to the beach as George flies ahead of you. He leads you around a cove and across a sandy dune. Finally, he lands on the top of a thick bush.

Exhausted from running, you lie down in the shade of the bush. Then George hops down and walks into a hole at the back of the bush.

A cave! you think.

Then you hear a mean, menacing voice say, "Get outta here, bird."

You wait. But George does not appear.

If you crawl under the bush and peek into the cave, turn to page 48.

If you think that the man sounds threatening, and you want to try to find help, turn to page 49.

You climb up to the cave but find that it is shallow and empty.

From the top of the hill, you can see all the way to the edge of town where there is a traveling carnival. You decide you would much rather go to the carnival than be all alone on the beach.

"Come on, George," you say happily, "let's go to the fair."

Turn to page 5.

Mrs. Crabbe gives you her flashlight, and you walk carefully down the old stone stairs. As soon as you are at the bottom, you hear the door above you slide closed.

"How dare you come here to meddle in my life!" Mrs. Crabbe screams through the panel. "The town has forgotten these stories, and I won't allow you to ruin everything for me just like Rachel ruined the good name of my ancestors."

You run up the stairs and try to slide open the panel. But it will not budge. Mrs. Crabbe has locked it. You bang on the door, but there is no answer.

You know that a long time ago there was another exit from this tunnel. You only hope you can find it before you are too weak to explore.

The End

"Did you say Papa John?" Mrs. Crabbe asks, alarmed. "That man at the junkyard?"

"Yes," you answer.

"You want to bring that man into my house? Over my dead body! He's dirty. He's creepy. And I won't have him here."

"Have you ever met him?" you ask.

"No," Mrs. Crabbe answers sheepishly.

"Well, it seems to me," you say, "that you're treating him just like those people treated your ancestor, Rachel, a long time ago."

Mrs. Crabbe stops. "You're right," she says thoughtfully. "Go get him and bring him here."

Turn to page 50.

"I refuse to eat until you tell me why you have brought me here," you say obstinately.

"It is not *you* we want," says the witch. "It is your bird. He is one of the rare ravens of Thunder Canyon, and we want to use his magic."

You did not realize until now that the witch had also grabbed George off the boat. You are shocked to see him perched on her arm.

If you are curious about George's powers, and you think you can learn about them from the witch, turn to page 52.

If you grab George and try to make a run for it, turn to page 53.

You take the bowl in your hands and then lift the spoon. It is filled with slimy globs and stringy things that look as if they might start to crawl.

"Eat it now," the witch orders.

You put the spoon in your mouth and swallow some of the broth. You feel a slithery sensation on your tongue, and the food slides down your throat. When you look at the witch again, you see four eyes instead of two, and two mouths instead of one. Everything in the room begins to whirl. Shapes and sounds blend as the room grows brighter. Then the light begins to dim, and you feel weaker and weaker. You feel yourself fading away until you are nothing. You wonder if this is what it is like to die.

The End

"Show me," you say with a grin, not believing her at all.

"Watch," she says as she points her finger to the sky. "King of Darkness, bring on the thunder!" she cries. The sky turns black, and the air is filled with thunder and lightning.

"Are you convinced?" she asks.

"Coincidence," you answer. "You read the weather report."

"Then watch this," she says as the gaming wheel spins in a booth next to you. The wheel stops and all the bettors cheer. "We won! Every one of us has won!" they cry with delight.

Turn to page 54.

You lean over the railing and motion for the clown to come closer.

"I think there's going to be a fire in this tent," you whisper. You are very careful not to let anyone else hear you because you do not want to cause a panic in the audience.

"Don't be silly!" the clown says laughingly. "I've worked in this tent for twenty-five years, and we've never had a fire."

George lands on your shoulder again, and this time the vision is even clearer: You see people stampeding, screaming, running mindlessly out of the tent. You know that you have to do something. If the clown will not believe you, you must go to someone of authority.

Then you think of the ringmaster.

Turn to page 57.

You go to the bandstand and look for signs of a fire; but there are none.

Then you turn to a group of clowns standing next to you and tell them what is going to happen.

"Some kinda nut," says one clown as he taps his head and makes a face.

"Please believe me!" you plead. "It's true! I know it!"

"Come on. Let's get away from this creep," another clown says. And they all walk away from you. There is only one clown left.

"I don't know if I believe you," says this one independent clown. "But I don't want to take a chance. Too many people could die if you are right."

Turn to page 59.

With George on your shoulder, you approach the house. It is surrounded by a high iron fence. You ring the bell next to a huge gate. There is a buzzing sound, and the gate opens automatically. As soon as you reach the front door it, too, opens. You wait for someone to appear, but all you can see is a hand on the doorknob. You cannot believe your eyes. The hand is not attached to an arm or a body. It is just a hand, working all by itself!

You peer inside the house. It is dark and foreboding, and you do not know what to do.

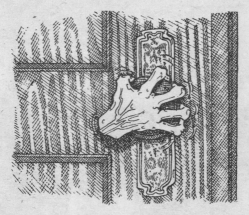

If you decide to get out of there as fast as you can, turn to page 60.

If you try to deliver the letter, turn to page 62.

You love driving the bumper cars and are having a terrific time crashing into others. George is riding on your shoulder, and you are laughing, when suddenly you hear a scream.

Just ahead of you, you see a small child who has fallen out of a bumper car and onto the floor. You are headed directly for him.

(continued on page 43)

Then, to your astonishment, George spreads his wings and flaps them three times. Every car in the hall comes to a sudden stop.

"I saw that! He's the bird that I'm looking for!" a man shouts.

You turn to see the same man who chased you in the Hall of Mirrors. The man starts running toward you.

Turn to page 63.

"Hurry up, kid," says Rocco. "We can't place a bet after the race begins."

That's it! you think. *I have to stall.*

You put your hand on your head and squint your eyes as if you are concentrating very hard. "It's coming . . ." you tell them. "It's coming. I see the beginning of a picture."

"Hurry!" Ratso says. "Maybe a knock on the head will make the picture come sooner. Huh, boss? Watcha think?"

A bell rings. The race has begun. It is too late to place a bet.

"Elmer!" you shout. "Elmer's the winner!"

The room is silent as you all listen to the race on the radio. "And Elmer wins by a length!" the announcer shouts.

(continued on page 45)

"You done it!" Ratso cheers. "You done it, kid! You picked the winner!"

"Hey, kid," says Rocco, "you may have been too late for this race, but I'll make sure you won't be too late for the next one."

Your heart sinks. All you want to do is get out of there.

"Here's ten bucks," Rocco says. "And there's another ten for every race you call."

"What time should I get here tomorrow?" you ask, knowing that once you get out of there, you will never come back.

"Tomorrow? Who said anything about tomorrow, kid? Did you say anything about tomorrow, Ratso?" Rocco asks in mock seriousness. "You don't unnerstand, kid. You ain't goin' nowhere. You're gonna be right here with us for a long, long time."

The End

You look over the list. "Batman!" you shout, crossing your fingers. "Batman's going to win!"

The men place their bets on Batman to win. You listen to the race, afraid of what they will do if Batman loses.

"And the winner is Elmer!" shouts the radio announcer.

"The kid's a fake!" says one of the men. "Throw him outta here!" says another.

"He can't go nowhere," Rocco says ominously. "He knows too much." Rocco looks at Ratso and orders, "Finish him off."

At that moment, George flies to the pile of money stacked in the middle of the floor. He flaps his wings furiously, and suddenly there is money everywhere, swirling all over the room.

The men race around, trying to gather up the money again. Everything and everyone is confused.

George lands on your shoulder, and you run out the door.

"Well done, George," you say as you rush through the candy store and straight to the police station.

The End

Crawling on your belly, you inch your way slowly toward the entrance to the cave. You are completely hidden by the bushes.

Just as you are about to creep out from under the bushes, you see two huge boots in front of your face.

If you reveal your presence to the man in the boots, turn to page 64.

If you stay perfectly still and hope that the man does not see you, turn to page 65.

You sneak away and run toward town. You have not gone far when you see a man.

"Help me!" you call out to him. "My pet raven crawled into a hidden cave back there. And when I started to go inside, I heard a very angry-sounding man. I need your help."

"That angry person you heard is my business partner," the man says, grabbing you. "Too bad you were in the wrong place at the wrong time, kid. Now you'll have to pay us a visit." He starts to drag you back to the cave. "Come and see our collection of jewels. We've stolen them from every house in town. I hope you like them, because you're going to be in that cave for a long, long time."

The End

As you are telling Papa John your story, George lands on your shoulder. Suddenly, you see a woman walk right through the room. She is dressed in a long, full evening gown.

"Who's that woman?" you ask, surprised to see someone so elegantly dressed walking around in Papa John's shack.

Astounded, Papa John asks, "You see her?"

"Of course I see her," you answer. "She was right next to me. She's beautiful. Who is she?"

"A ghost," Papa John answers matter-of-factly. "Her home was built on this spot over a hundred years ago. She frequently comes back for a visit. You and I are the only ones who have ever seen her."

(continued on page 51)

"But doesn't it scare you to have a ghost in your house?" you ask.

"'Course not. She's very friendly," Papa John answers casually. "She's not exactly a ghost, by the way. She's a revenant."

"What's that?"

"It's a spirit caught between two worlds because of some unresolved problem," he explains. "It seems that her family heirlooms were stolen from her when she was a child, and she never received her inheritance. She'll not rest until she finds the jewels."

Suddenly, George flaps his wings frantically and flies out the door.

If you want to follow George, turn to page 66.

If you would rather take Papa John and show him the tunnel in Mrs. Crabbe's house, turn to page 67.

"Are you really a witch?" you ask.

"Yes. But this is just a costume for the House of Horrors. No self-respecting witch would be caught dead wearing such a silly get-up in this day and age," the witch answers.

"What do witches do?" you ask.

"Oh, cast spells, mix potions, work magic . . . routine stuff. We'd like to do more, but our magic is limited. That's why we want the raven. He will help us expand our powers considerably. He's very valuable, you know."

"What can he do?"

"Almost anything, once you catch on to how to work his magic," the witch answers.

If you ask for a demonstration of the witch's powers, turn to page 68.

If you ask to see a demonstration of George's powers, turn to page 69.

You grab George and start to run. But the witch grabs you by the hair and demands to know your name.

"It's Piggy," you say. "My name is Piggy."

She picks up a knife from the table and cuts off a lock of your hair.

As you run to the door, she holds the hair toward the fire. "May the fires of life burn a curse on Piggy before nightfall. May Piggy be run over by a car!" she screams.

You run out of the witch's lair, holding George and smiling to yourself. You know that a witch must know the name of the victim in order to lay a proper curse. And you did not give her your real name.

The End

"Just good luck," you say, still unconvinced.

"Try this one on for size," she says with a wicked gleam in her eyes. "The next roller coaster that comes around that curve is going to fly right off the track."

Trembling, you stare at the roller coaster. Suddenly, you are very frightened.

"No!" you cry. "Don't do it!"

Ignoring you in her desire to prove her magic, the witch looks at the roller coaster and says, "King of Darkness, invoke your powers!"

(continued on page 55)

You hear the roller coaster coming. Then you see the first car round the bend. And, to your horror, it starts to leave the tracks, taking all the other cars with it.

Just then, George flies onto the witch's shoulder and flaps his wings slowly three times. Without even jerking, the roller coaster returns to the track.

(continued on page 56)

"My magic!" the witch screams, shaking her hand at the raven. "Your power has ruined my magic!"

She stamps her feet and shakes her fist, then she runs angrily back into the tunnel.

You look at George with awe and wonder if he really is a magical bird. You are not at all certain you trust your eyes. *There is no way to know,* you think.

George follows you as you walk toward the bumper cars. This is your favorite ride, and you are excited about trying it out.

As you approach the ticket booth, you see a woman who is crying.

If you would rather not get involved with the crying woman, turn to page 70.

If you stop to inquire whether you can help the woman, turn to page 71

You make your way through the crowd, pushing and shoving in your haste to get to the ringmaster.

The trapeze artists are swinging over your head as you dodge among the elephants. You bump into a juggler, causing him to drop his bowling pins.

"Stop that kid!" a clown yells. "Get that kid out of here!"

Someone grabs you just as you reach the ringmaster.

"Fire!" you whisper desperately. "There's going to be a fire in here!"

"Get this kid out of here!" the ringmaster shouts.

Just then, George swoops out of the air and lands on your shoulder. Hoping that the magic is transferable, you quickly take the raven and place him on the ringmaster's shoulder.

(continued on page 58)

As soon as George is on his shoulder, the ringmaster cries out, "Oh, no!" And you know that he, too, has seen the vision.

"What is this?" the ringmaster asks accusingly. "Some kind of magic spell? Get that bird out of here! He's bad luck!"

If you stay and try to convince the ringmaster to believe in George's powers, turn to page 72.

If you try to convince someone else about the fire, turn to page 73.

"I have a plan," the clown says. "I'm in the fire brigade skit. It's usually a joke, but this time I'll attach the hose to the real hydrant instead of a fake. If there *is* a fire, I'll be able to put it out."

If you go with the clown to ride on the fire engine, turn to page 76.

If you want to stay near the bandstand so that you can spot the fire the minute it starts, turn to page 78.

You run back down the path to the huge gate; but it is locked, and you cannot escape. You grab the fence and start to climb. Suddenly, you feel a jolt of electricity penetrate your body.

(continued on page 61)

When you wake up, you are in a bed. The room is dark. When your eyes adjust to the darkness, you see a huge monster standing beside the bed. His buck teeth shine when he grins at you. Soft brown fur covers his chubby body.

Terrified, you stare at him, not knowing what to do.

If you think that you should try to talk to the monster, turn to page 80.

If you think you should try to get out of there as fast as you can, turn to page 81.

Not knowing what else to do, you look at the hand and speak to it. "Excuse me," you say, "I have a letter to deliver. Will you take it?"

The hand beckons you inside. You enter, and the door closes behind you, shutting out George.

You follow the hand down a long hall, still not believing your eyes.

Then the hand opens a door and nudges you into a room.

Across the room there is a big fat man sitting behind a desk.

"How nice of you to come," he says with a smile. "Sit down," he invites, indicating a chair in front of his desk.

If you sit in the chair, turn to page 82.

If you tell the man you just want to give him the letter and then leave, turn to page 83.

Before you can get away, the man grabs you. Then he pushes the barrel of a gun into your back and orders you to walk quietly away from the crowds.

The man takes you behind a tent, where you are alone with him.

"Don't worry," he says, putting away his gun. "It's not you I want. It's your bird."

"But why?" you ask.

"Because I have it on good authority that there is treasure buried near here. I know that your bird has magical powers and can help me find it. If you'll cooperate, I'll split the treasure with you."

If you like the idea of becoming rich, turn to page 84.

If you refuse to go anywhere with this stranger, turn to page 85.

Peering out from your hiding place on the ground, you say, "Excuse me, sir."

The man looks down, grabs you by the arm and pulls you to a standing position.

"What are you doing here?" he demands in a gruff, threatening voice.

If you answer that the beach is free and that you have a right to be there, turn to page 87.

If you tell the man that you only want to catch your pet bird and then leave, turn to page 88.

You wait patiently until the man goes inside. Then you creep away. Soon, George joins you, and the two of you explore another cave way up at the top of the hill.

At the back of this new cave, you crawl through a tiny opening and find yourself in a long, dark tunnel. Near the end of this tunnel, you shine your flashlight into another opening. You are shocked to discover a pile of human bones, skull and all.

It's the girl! you think. *The one who wrote the diary.*

Just then, George lands on your shoulder, and you have an awful vision of rocks falling and dirt caving in.

If you think that this vision is a warning, turn to page 89.

If you want to stay in the cave and explore a little more, turn to page 90.

As you follow, George flies to a tall pine tree at the edge of the junkyard. Then he lands on a big mound of rubbish and flaps his wings.

You dig through the rubbish, but all you find at the bottom is a pile of old bricks.

You are exhausted from the digging and disappointed that you have found nothing. You may go home now and get a good night's sleep. You hope that George will lead you to something more exciting tomorrow.

The End

If you think you have enough energy left, turn to page 67 and go with Papa John to explore the tunnel.

It is damp and cold in the tunnel, and you can hear rats scuttling across the stone floors. You explore with Papa John for over two hours, but you find no trace of Rachel, the girl who wrote the diary.

Just as you are about to give up, George lands on your shoulder. Suddenly, you see two small openings in the wall.

If you crawl through the opening on the right, turn to page 91.

If you crawl through the opening on the left, turn to page 92.

"Show me your stuff," you say cynically to the witch.

Then, without a word, she picks up a doll and sticks a pin into the doll's hand. Suddenly, you feel a sharp pain in *your* hand.

"That's incredible!" you say, wide-eyed.

"Elementary, my dear," says the witch, "but good enough for a trial run."

"Can you fly?" you ask.

"Of course not. It's just a myth that witches toot all over the place on broomsticks. We cast our spells and do our magic in less obvious ways. But I cannot tell you any more unless you become one of us."

"How can I do that?" you inquire.

"All you have to do to become a member of our coven is drink the brew from the cauldron."

If you decide to drink, turn to page 94.

If you refuse, turn to page 95.

"Show me what George can really do," you say, challenging the witch.

"I don't know all of his powers," she answers. "We witches and warlocks have a lot to learn. That is why we want him."

"But George belongs to me. He's my pet. You can't have him," you declare.

"But I already *do* have him," she answers with a wicked grin. "Finders keepers . . ."

"Never!" you scream at her.

If you grab George from her arm and try to make a run for it, turn to page 96.

If you wait to see if George's magic will get you out of this terrible situation, turn to page 97.

You buy your ticket for the bumper car ride and step inside.

You are thinking how nice it is to have George as a companion, when he takes off from your shoulder and flies away.

"George!" you yell. "Come back, George!"

Circling above you, George flies higher and higher. Suddenly, you know, without being told, that you will never see your raven again. You wish now that you had stopped to help that woman in trouble.

The End

You stop next to the woman. "May I help you?" you inquire.

"My little girl!" the woman answers. "She's lost! And no one can find her."

George is sitting on your shoulder. He turns his head toward the woman and flaps his wings three times. Then he flies away.

"Follow my raven," you say to the woman. "He might be able to help you."

Suddenly, George swoops down and lands near the fortune-telling booth. There, sitting on a chair eating cotton candy, is the little lost girl.

"Suzanne!" the mother screams as she hugs her child. Tears of joy fall onto her cheeks.

"Thank you so much," she says to you and George. "Thank you. Both of you are heroes."

The End

If you want to continue your adventures at the carnival and go to the Fun House, turn to page 11.

You tell the ringmaster about your Uncle George and how he sent you the magic raven. But nothing you say can convince him. You think how sad it is that some people will never believe in magic, even when it is right under their nose.

"Forget it!" you yell at the ringmaster as you run from him. "I'll talk to the bandleader."

(continued on page 73)

You run to the bandleader and place George on his shoulder. You can see from the expression on the man's face that he sees the vision.

"We cannot let this happen," the bandleader says. "But how will we prevent it?"

You think desperately for a moment, trying to find a solution. "I know!" you cry. "Form a marching band."

(continued on page 74)

He follows your directions. Then you take charge of the microphone. "Ladies and gentlemen!" you announce. "We are now going to do something unprecedented in the history of the circus. We are all going to march through the midway of the carnival. Strike up the band! Bring on the elephants and the tigers!" you shout.

(continued on page 75)

As the band plays, you direct the audience to file out of the tent, section by section. They are all having a wonderful time, waving their balloons and marching with the animals and the clowns.

As the last row files out, you see the flames. In a few minutes, the entire tent is consumed by a raging fire.

You are sorry that the tent will be destroyed. But you are proud that you have saved the lives of hundreds of people and animals. Congratulations. You are a hero.

The End

You wish that you could enjoy the fire-engine ride. You want to wave to the crowd, but all you can do is look for a fire.

Suddenly, you see sparks coming from an electrical wire. The wire is stretched across a pile of hay. Before you can alert the clown, the hay catches on fire.

"There!" you shout to the clown.

He sees the flames and aims his hose at the fire. And then he stops.

"I can't put water on an electrical fire. It's too dangerous. I don't know what to do," the clown says to you.

(continued on page 77)

"I'll get the wire out of the way!" you shout.

You run over and grab hold of the wire where it is safely covered with the rubber coating. Then you pull it away from the hay and onto the concrete.

"Now!" you shout. And the clown douses the burning hay with his hose.

Everyone in the audience thinks that you are part of the act. They all laugh when the clown puts out the fire.

Afterward, the clown puts his arm around your shoulders.

"Those hundreds of people will never know that you saved their lives," he says. "It would frighten them to know that there was a real fire here. But I know that you're a hero. And I'm sure you know that, too."

The End

The main event begins, but you see none of it. Instead, you walk around the bandstand, circling it slowly time and again, looking for a fire.

Just when you are about to give up, you see a spark, then another and another.

The sparks are coming from a frayed electrical wire that is lying on top of a pile of hay. You know that the hay could burst into flames at any second.

(continued on page 79)

You follow the wire with your eyes. It leads under the bandstand and connects to a small generator.

You run around the stand and pull out the plug. One of the giant lights goes out, but the sparks stop. You cut the wire in two with your pocketknife to make certain it cannot be connected again.

You breathe a sigh of relief, but then you feel a hand clamp down on your shoulder.

"Get outta here," a man says. "You don't belong here."

Confident that the people are safe, you make your way back to your seat. You feel sad and disappointed that no one noticed the fact that you saved the lives of hundreds of people.

Oh, well, you think to yourself finally, *I suppose that's not the first good deed that has gone unrecognized.*

The End

Your voice trembles as you ask, "Who are you? What are you doing here?"

"I'm a guard monster," he answers with a tinge of pride. "They told me to bring you to them as soon as you woke up."

"To whom?" you ask.

"Follow me, and you'll see."

Turn to page 98.

You jump off the bed and start to run toward the door. But you have taken only a few steps when you feel the monster's enormous, hairy, clawed paw on your neck.

He holds on to you and he grins. Then, licking his lips, he says, "Gotcha!"

The End

You sit down in the chair. But before your behind touches the seat, the chair moves away. You plop with a thump on the floor.

"Ha ha ha!" the man laughs, his belly shaking. "You fell for it!

"Here," he says, "let me help you up."

You take his hand, and you feel a buzzing shock. The man laughs even harder. "See this ring?" he asks. You look at the deep green emerald on his pinky finger, and it squirts water in your eyes.

You think this man is a terrible practical joker and wish you could get away from his silliness.

"Tell you what I'm gonna do," the man says. "Here are two boxes. Inside one is the key that will unlock the door to your freedom. Inside the other is a surprise."

You look at the boxes.

"Do you want the red box or the blue one?" he asks with a wicked twinkle in his eyes.

If you choose the red box, turn to page 99.

If you choose the blue box, turn to page 100.

"I just want to deliver this envelope and then leave," you tell the man as politely as you can.

"Sit down!" he orders.

But you shake your head no.

"Nobody defies me!" the man bellows. "Tinker Bell! Come in here! On the double!" he yells.

You wait to see who will enter. When the door opens, you're not at all pleased. Standing before you is a monster who is half cow and half man. He is covered with scales, except for the curly blond hair that surrounds his ugly face.

"Take him away, Tinker Bell," the man orders. "Take him away now!"

The End

As you walk to the beach with the man, he tells you about the pirates who buried treasure here many years ago.

George leads the way, but the closer you get to the water, the higher he flies.

"He's leaving us!" the man yells. "Do something!"

But there is nothing you can do. George disappears into the clouds.

You feel saddened by the loss of your raven, and you do not even pay attention to the man.

Suddenly, you feel the pistol once again as the man shoves it into your back.

"Come with me—now," he orders with a grin. "Ransom is another kind of treasure, and I aim to get some."

The End

You are intrigued by the idea of finding treasure, but you know better than to go anywhere with a stranger.

"I can't go with you," you answer.

"Then give me the bird," the man orders.

"Never!" you reply as you start to run.

George leads the way.

"If I can't have him, no one will!" the man yells. He raises his gun and shoots at George. Miraculously, you see the bullet pass right through the raven, but nothing happens. George continues to fly as if the bullet had never touched him.

The man is so astounded that he stops chasing you, but you do not stop running until you reach your secret hideout: a flat rock on a hill overlooking the ocean.

(continued on page 86)

But your rock is not unoccupied. There is a man sitting on it.

He smiles gently and says, "I have been waiting for you."

"What do you want?" you ask.

"I have come for the raven."

"Please don't take him. Everyone wants to steal him."

"I did not come to steal him," the man replies. "I am from Thunder Canyon. And I come because, ever since the day we allowed your uncle to send the raven to you, my tribe has been plagued with bad luck. There is illness among my people. The rains pour down so hard that the crops do not grow. The river swells dangerously with raging waters; the children and old people grow weak.

"I know this is difficult for you, but I ask you humbly to return the raven so we can once again live in harmony with ourselves and with nature."

If you give George to the Indian, turn to page 101.

If you explain to him that you cannot give up a pet you have grown to love so dearly, turn to page 103.

"There's nothing wrong with my being here," you answer. "I have just as much of a right to be on this beach as you do."

"A smart alec, huh?" the man says, squeezing your arm tighter.

Just then, George flies out of the cave. Hanging from his claws are gold chains and bracelets, a string of pearls and a diamond necklace.

"Hey!" the man yells, pulling out a gun and aiming it at George.

If you try to hit the man's arm in order to keep him from shooting at George, turn to page 104.

If you kick the man and try to knock him off-balance, turn to page 105.

"I'm just looking for my pet raven," you explain to the man. "And then I have to go home."

Just then, George lands on your shoulder, and you see a picture of the inside of the cave in your head. There are jewels everywhere, and you realize that they are the loot from all the robberies that have been taking place in town.

"Here comes my bird now," you say to the man as casually as possible. "I'll be on my way home now."

If you trust the vision enough to go straight to the police, turn to page 106.

If you want to hide out and explore the cave when the man leaves, turn to page 107.

You trust what you have seen and run down the tunnel as quickly as you can. As you crawl through the tiny opening at the end, you hear an ominous rumble.

Pebbles begin to fall on your head, and a roar fills the cavern.

You do not stop running until you have escaped. Then you turn and watch as the cave collapses.

Your heart is still pounding when you give George a gentle, thankful hug.

The End

You decide that it would take just a little more time to inspect the pile of bones. When you lift up the skull, you see something gleaming underneath. It is a black enamel brooch in the shape of a raven in flight. There are two diamonds for eyes.

You are so engrossed in the brooch that you pay no attention to the rumble in the background.

When you return to the entrance of the tunnel, you discover that there has been an avalanche in the cave. Your exit is blocked.

You know that your flashlight will soon grow dim, and you hope that the magic of the raven will help you find another way out.

The End

You crawl through the opening on the right, and Papa John follows. Once inside, you swing your flashlight in an arc around the room.

Suddenly, the light lands on something.

"Ahhghhh!" you scream.

Turn to page 108.

You crawl through the tiny opening on the left. You are in a small room. You shine your light on the wall and see something stuck in between some stones; it is a diary written by Rachel. You begin to read:

"It is over. I have been locked in this tunnel with only five candles and food to last a few days. They also left me this diary so that I could write.

"They accused me of witchcraft, of casting spells. All I did was tell them where they could find Elizabeth Butler's stolen jewels.

"How did I know? you ask. I knew because I saw it in a vision. I saw the man take the jewels and hide them in the pine-tree well. I saw it all in my mind.

"It was foolish of me to have told the sheriff that I saw it in a vision. All I wanted him to do was check the well.

"But I frightened him with my knowledge. And he accused me publicly of being a witch.

(continued on page 93)

"The town turned against me. They called me the Raven Witch and sealed me in this tomb to await my fate.

"My only comfort is that the man who stole the jewels died a mysterious death on the day that I was accused.

"And now, this is the end. From my grave, I appeal to future generations to clear my name. I cannot rest in peace until that is done.

"Farewell. God be with you."

You and Papa John are stunned.

"The revenant in my shack is Elizabeth Butler," Papa John says. "Those are her jewels."

If you take Rachel's diary to the publisher of the town newspaper so that you can clear her name, you may end the story here.

The End

If you would rather search for the pine-tree well, turn to page 109.

You take the cup and drink. Suddenly, the shadows in the room start to move. The light of the fire turns brighter and brighter until you can see nothing else.

"Your first assignment in beginning-witch-craft is to bring us a dead cat," the witch orders.

"But where do I find a dead cat?" you ask.

"You don't *find* it. You catch it and kill it, of course."

"But I can't do that," you protest.

"It is your responsibility," the witch replies. "You chose to become one of us. You cannot back out now. It is too late."

"But I simply cannot do it," you say.

"Then you cannot live," says the witch.

The End

"I don't want to be a member of your coven," you tell the witch.

"You must," she replies. "You know too much. Either drink the broth or die!"

"No! I won't drink it!" you scream.

Suddenly, George flies to the middle of the room and flaps his wings very slowly three times. Immediately, all the witches and warlocks become silent. Then you notice that they do not move. They seem to be under some strange spell that has frozen them in place.

George flies toward you, circles your head and goes out the door. You follow him, awed by his power and grateful for the spell that has saved your life.

The End

You lunge toward the witch, grab George and begin to run.

Without any panic, the witch reaches for the voodoo doll that hangs from a cord around her neck. She plunges a pin through the stomach of the doll.

You feel an agonizing pain in your own stomach, and you know that you will never see sunlight again.

The End

George sits quietly on the witch's arm. He looks around and then stares intently at the fire as he flaps his wings very slowly three times.

Suddenly, the fire is extinguished, and the room is plunged into darkness.

"What happened?" cries a witch on the other side of the room.

"I can't see!" yells a warlock.

You hear a whirring of wings in the darkness, and then you feel George's claws grip your finger. He tugs at you, and you follow.

He leads you out of the House of Horrors and into the sunlight. You are very happy that you can go home now.

The End

If you do not want to go home and would rather visit the Fun House, turn to page 11.

You follow the monster as he lumbers awkwardly down the hall. He is so clumsy that you want to laugh. He takes you into a room, and when you look around, you are horrified. Everywhere you look, there are hands and feet, legs and heads floating in midair. An occasional torso drifts by as you stare. The sight is revolting, the most nauseating thing you have ever seen.

"Where is the raven?" asks a head that has no body.

"I've got it in here," the monster answers as he lets George out of a paper bag.

"What are you going to do?" you ask, your eyes wide with fear.

"*We're* not going to do anything," says another head. "*You're* going to use your raven's powers to make us whole again."

Without warning, George flies across the room. He dodges in and out among the body parts as he makes his way to the light switch. His wing grazes the switch, and suddenly, the room is dark.

If you think George has darkened the room so that you can make a run for it, turn to page 112.

If you think George is using his powers to unite all the bodies, turn to page 113.

You pick up the red box and open it. Inside is a large ornate key.

"Darn it!" says the man. "You chose the key."

"What's it for?" you ask.

"The front gate," he answers. "Now get outta here before I change my mind and make you open the other box."

You say thank you and hurry out of the house. You are grateful when you discover the key really does fit the lock on the gate. And when George flies onto your shoulder, you know you are safe.

The End

You look at the blue box, wondering what kind of joke this is. You open the top and reach inside. But this is no joke, you realize too late. Your hand is covered with stinging sensations.

When you lift your hand out, it is covered with small African scorpions.

"Ha ha!" the man roars. "Some joke, huh?"

You cannot believe your eyes as you try to shake off the long-tailed creatures.

"You can go now," the man says with a wicked gleam in his eyes. "Just how far you go is up to you. The African scorpions' poison is deadly, and it works fast."

If you run as quickly as you can out of the house, turn to page 114.

If you remain calm and walk out of the house, turn to page 115.

"I will give him to you," you answer with tears in your eyes. "I will miss him, but perhaps someday I can visit Thunder Canyon and see George again."

"Thank you," the Indian says as he reaches out and touches you gently on the cheek. "I shall take the raven. But I shall not take all his magic. You have within you the power to see and hear things differently. It exists in all of us. We simply have to learn how to use it. It requires faith in yourself and patience with the passage of time. Always remember that.

"Wherever you are, whatever you are doing, you shall forever have a home with my people in Thunder Canyon."

The End ___

"I cannot give him to you," you say. "George has grown too precious to me."

"Then you need not give him to me," the Indian answers softly. "We shall let the raven decide. I shall leave now. If the raven follows me, you must allow him to go. If he stays with you, then you are the possessor of a true treasure."

The sun is low in the sky as the Indian climbs down the hill. The air is still, and the clouds are colored with flame.

You stand on your rock and look at George. He looks at you, then flies over and lands on your shoulder. Brushing your cheek once with his enormous wing, he hesitates and then flies after the Indian.

You watch as he grows smaller and smaller, his shining feathers silhouetted against the twilight sky. Finally, he blends into the light.

The End

You hit the man's arm and knock the gun out of his hand. Then you pick up the gun.

"I suppose you're the burglar who is responsible for all the robberies in town," you say.

The man looks at the gun in your hand and raises his arms over his head.

"Don't shoot!" he pleads.

"Start walking," you order as you gesture with the gun. "It's a long walk to the police station."

The End

You swing your leg back and kick the man in the shins with all your might.

The kick causes him to miss George, but he grabs you.

"Now you're really in trouble," he says. "Get into the cave."

He pushes you inside. You are amazed at what you see. The floor and walls are lined with silver and gold objects. You realize that this man is the burglar who has been robbing all the houses in town.

You want to do something, but the man binds your legs tightly and ties your hands behind your back. Then he leaves.

If you use the sharp edge of the rock in the corner to try to file through your ropes, turn to page 116.

If you try to loosen the knots in the rope by wiggling your hands, turn to page 117.

It takes you a while to convince the police that the jewels are in the cave. But they finally decide to investigate your claim.

When they discover you are right, you are given a huge reward.

Your picture is on the front page of the paper that same day, and the entire town turns out to celebrate. Everybody calls you a hero.

The End

You hide out until you see the man leave. Then you creep into the cave.

Suddenly, you feel two hands grab you around the neck. You never even considered the possibility that the man might have a partner inside the cave. It is a serious oversight on your part.

The End

There, glowing in the light, is a pile of bones. And at the top of the pile is a human skull, the teeth gleaming.

"That must be the remains of Rachel," says Papa John, lowering his head in respect.

You decide to go tell Mrs. Crabbe what you have found.

Just as you are crawling out, you notice something sparkling on the floor. You pick it up and see that it is a black enamel brooch. It is fashioned in the shape of a raven in flight, with two small diamonds for eyes.

You take the raven brooch and call to Mrs. Crabbe. She meets you at the door of the tunnel. As soon as she sees the brooch, her eyes glare at you and her mouth hardens.

"I cannot allow you to stir up this shame from the past!" she screams. "You will ruin my name!"

And, before you can stop her, she slides the door closed, locking you and Papa John in the tunnel.

The End

You hurry back to the shack with Papa John.

"I know where they are!" Papa John announces excitedly to the invisible presence in a corner of the room. "The jewels are in the pine-tree well. Can you think of where that would be?"

"I can't see the ghost," you say to Papa John, crushed that you have lost your special sight.

Just then, George flies in and lands on your shoulder. Suddenly, you see the ghost again; she is lovely and elegant in her long silk gown. You hear her say: "My friend Rachel was with me when I planted a pine tree by our well for my twelfth birthday. Come, I'll show you."

(continued on page 110)

You hurry outside and follow Elizabeth as she floats toward a giant pine tree near the edge of the junkyard. "Well, I'll be," Papa John says. "It's right under our noses."

"The well used to be right here," Elizabeth says, pointing to a pile of bricks.

You and Papa John work hard at removing the bricks. Then you lift a huge piece of sheet metal and discover the remains of a well.

Papa John gets some rope from the shack and lowers you into the well. When you reappear, you are holding a metal box in your hands. The box is filled to the brim with precious jewels.

(continued on page 111)

"Part of the Butler family still lives in town," Papa John says thoughtfully. "We must take the jewels to them."

You do just that, and each of you is rewarded with a huge diamond. But you do not tell the Butler family about the ghost named Elizabeth. You do not want to be called crazy heroes.

The End

You run in the direction of the door and immediately step on a random foot. You hear a head cry, "Ouch!" in another part of the room.

Just as you reach the door, you feel seven hands grab you.

"I've got the kid!" says one head. "No, I do!" argues another, who is convinced it is his hand that is holding you back.

"I think we all do," says a third.

"No matter," says another head as a lone hand waves casually in the air. "The kid is ours now, to make a part of us."

All the heads laugh. But you do not think the joke is very funny.

The End

It is dark. Everyone is silent. The only noise you hear is the flapping of George's wings. Then he squeals and crows. Finally, there is a strange, haunting cry as George flips on the lights.

There is a stunned silence, and you can see again. The room is filled with ten people who can do nothing except stare at each other in wonder.

"The raven has broken the spell!" someone shouts in jubilation.

"Humpty Dumpty has nothing on us!" cries another. "Finally, we're whole again!"

"Quick," says a woman who appears to be the leader. "Let's get out of here before the Fat Man finds out."

You do not bother to ask who she means. You just run out of there with the rest of them, grateful that you can escape.

The End

You start to run. You do not understand that the strenuous exercise makes your blood circulate faster, carrying the poison around your body at a much quicker rate.

When you reach the front gate, it swings open automatically. You feel yourself grow faint. You grab hold of the gate. But it is too late. You feel yourself growing fainter and know that soon you will die.

The End

You walk slowly out of the house, knowing that running will make your poisoned blood circulate faster. You try to remain calm so that the poison will not reach your heart too quickly.

You see the fire station only two blocks away. You try to keep on walking, but you fall to the ground. Your head begins to spin. Then your body feels lighter, as if gravity has disappeared and invisible arms are lifting you.

You feel no fear, only an incredible sense of freedom and floating.

Suddenly, you feel as if you are being swept through a long corridor. At the end of this soft and dreamlike journey, you enter into a field of brilliant white light.

"Welcome," says a voice.

Turn to page 118.

You wiggle across the cave and position your wrists over the rock. Then you begin to move your hands back and forth over the sharp edge.

You have almost cut through the rope when the man returns.

"Caught you!" he says with an evil smile. "You won't get out of here alive."

The End

You wiggle your hands industriously and patiently for half an hour, but you cannot seem to loosen the knots. They are tied too tightly.

Even though you feel it is hopeless, you continue to work.

More than an hour later, you hear a flapping noise; suddenly, George is beside you. He walks behind your back and begins to peck at the knots. You know that if you had not been working to loosen the ropes all this time, they would have been too tight for George to untie.

Soon, the rope around your hands comes loose. You bend over and untie the rope that is binding your legs.

Peeking out of the cave, you see that the robber is nowhere in sight.

You stand up and begin to run, and you don't stop until you have reached the police station.

The End

Ahead of you, through clouds of mist, a person stands alone with arms outstretched toward you.

"Who are you?" you ask, feeling the warmth of the welcome.

"I am your guide," the person says in a gentle and musical voice.

"Where will you take me?"

"Over there, across the river," the guide replies.

You look at the river. Never in your life have you seen water so clear and shining, as if it were made of pure liquid crystal.

If you want to cross the river with the guide, turn to page 119.

If you think that it is not yet your time to cross the river, turn to page 120.

The guide reaches out and takes your hand, then he leads you to the river. You are surrounded by a new kind of beauty.

You feel no fear, only a wisp of sadness at what you have left behind.

The End

Although you do not understand why, you cannot go with the guide. And you express this with a simple gesture of your head.

The guide smiles and then begins to fade into the light.

You watch as firemen work to save your life. It is as if you are floating above your body, looking at yourself.

You watch as they discover one of the African scorpions that is caught on the sleeve of your shirt. The firemen make an emergency call for anti-venom.

You drift in a timeless space until you hear a fireman say, "Put the mask over his face; he's coming around."

You feel unaccountably sad that you have left the crystal river behind you. And yet, you know that you have been saved, and you are grateful for your life.

You open your eyes and smile. George is standing next to you.

The End